Pony-Crazed Princess

Princess Ellie Solves a Mystery

Read all the adventures of Princess Ellie!

Pony-Crazed Princess

Princess Ellie Solves a Mystery

by Diana Kimpton

Illustrated by Lizzie Finlay

Hyperion Paperbacks for Children
New York

For Graham

First published in the United Kingdom in 2005 as
The Pony-Mad Princess: Princess Ellie and the Palace Plot
by Usborne Publishing Ltd.
Based on an original concept by Anne Finnis
Text copyright © 2005 by Diana Kimpton and Anne Finnis
Illustrations copyright © 2005 by Lizzie Finlay

Printed in the United States of America
First U.S. edition, 2007
1 3 5 7 9 10 8 6 4 2

This book is set in 14.5-point Nadine Normal.

ISBN-13: 978-14231-0901-3
ISBN-10: 1-4231-0901-5

Visit www.hyperionbooksforchildren.com

Chapter 1

"Come on, Angel," said Princess Ellie, patting the skewbald foal's brown-and-white neck. Angel's tiny hooves crunched on the gravel as she walked up the palace drive. Ellie was on one side of the foal, and her best friend, Kate, was on the other.

Kate grinned. "She's getting a lot better at being led." She held up the lead rope to show Ellie how slack it was. "Look at this!

She's not even pulling at all."

"We could try going faster," suggested Ellie. "But that's up to you. She's your pony."

Kate made a clicking noise with her tongue and started to run. Angel pricked up her ears, arched her neck, and broke into a trot.

Suddenly, Ellie heard the sound of an engine. She looked around quickly and saw a bright red sports car racing up behind them. She waved at it to slow down, but the driver just waved back. He didn't adjust his speed at all. Ellie waved again, more urgently this time. Angel was only a foal. She wasn't used to traffic.

But the driver still took no notice. He gave

a long, loud blast on the car's horn. Then he roared past, waving cheerfully. The wheels of the red car sent up a shower of gravel.

The combination of the noise, the speed, and the stinging stones was too much for Angel. She jumped away from the car, nearly knocking Kate over. Then she threw herself backward, pulling hard on the rope and trying to break free.

Ellie lunged forward and grabbed hold of Angel's halter. "Steady, girl," she said in a soothing voice. "It's okay now."

"There, there, don't be afraid," added Kate, gently stroking the foal's face.

Angel relaxed a little. She stopped trying to pull away, but she was obviously still scared. She was breathing fast, and her neck was damp with sweat.

3

There was no sign of the car now. It had sped away toward the palace and disappeared around a corner. Ellie glowered after it. "That was rude! I wonder who he is."

Kate looked thoughtful. "The guards at the gate let him in, so he must be visiting someone at the palace."

"That's true," replied Ellie. "But he obviously doesn't know anything about horses, or he wouldn't have frightened Angel."

Kate turned the foal toward the stable. "Let's get out of the way quickly, before he comes back."

Meg, the palace groom, was sweeping the yard when Ellie and Kate arrived. She stopped as soon as she saw them. "How did Angel's lesson go?" she asked.

She listened with concern as Ellie and Kate described what had happened. "Thank goodness Angel wasn't hurt," she said when they had finished.

"She could have been, if she'd gotten away," said Kate. "She was really scared."

"But she's calmed down now," said Ellie. "Should we put her out in the field with Starlight?"

"That's a good idea," said Meg. "She'll be pleased to be back with her mom."

Starlight whinnied a welcome and trotted to the gate to meet her daughter. As soon as Kate had unfastened Angel's halter, the two of them cantered side by side to their favorite spot in the shade of an oak tree. Starlight was the largest of Ellie's five ponies, but Angel's spindly legs were so long that she was easily able to keep up with her mother.

The other four ponies were standing on the far side of the field, swishing their tails gently to keep the flies away. Shadow, the greedy Shetland, was the only one eating the grass. His best friend, Sundance, dozed beside him, while Moonbeam and Rainbow stood side by side, watching Angel.

Suddenly a polite cough made Ellie jump, and a deep voice said, "Excuse me, Princess Aurelia."

She spun around and saw Higginbottom, the butler, standing behind her. She'd been so busy watching the ponies that she hadn't heard him approaching.

Higginbottom gave a deep bow. As usual, he was wearing his black evening suit and white gloves. She had never seen him in any other clothes, and she had never been able to persuade him to call her Ellie. Like everyone else at the palace, he insisted on calling her by her formal name.

He straightened up and announced, "The King and Queen would like you to join them for tea in the parlor as soon as possible. The new royal designer has arrived, and they want you to meet him."

Ellie groaned. Why now? she thought. She hated having to cut short her time at the stable. "But I was going to clean Starlight's saddle before supper," she said.

"It'll be all right," said Kate. "It can wait until tomorrow. And the royal designer might be interesting. I wonder what he's going to design?"

"I haven't heard anything," replied Ellie. She suddenly felt very curious to find out. "Okay, let's go."

As the girls approached the palace, Ellie saw a parked red sports car and remembered the rude driver who had scared Angel.

I hope he's not the designer, she thought. She'd already seen enough of that man for one day.

Chapter 2

Ellie ran through the front door and nearly bumped into her governess.

"Where are you going in such a rush?" asked Miss Stringle.

"To the parlor," explained Ellie. "Mom and Dad told me to be there to meet the new designer."

Miss Stringle was unimpressed. "That is no reason to run. There is always time for a princess to walk in a dignified manner." She paused and wrinkled her nose in disgust. "And there's always time to change out of your riding clothes."

Ellie sighed. No one else in the palace seemed to like the smell of horse as much as she did. She walked sedately up the spiral staircase to her room until she was out of Miss Stringle's sight. Then she ran up the remaining steps, two at a time.

Inside her very pink bedroom, she pulled off her riding clothes and wiped the dirt off her face with a wet towel. Then she put on a frilly pink dress, swapped her everyday crown for a formal tiara, and hurried down to the parlor.

Despite her rush, she couldn't resist stopping at a small table beside the double doors. Resting in the middle of the table was her favorite ornament—a beautiful gold statue of a flying horse. Its glittering wings were encrusted with diamonds, and its eyes were clear blue sapphires.

She gazed admiringly at it for a moment. Then she forced herself to turn away. Her parents were waiting for her, and she didn't want to get into trouble by being late. She smoothed the front of her skirt, swung open the doors, and stepped into the parlor.

The King and Queen smiled at her as she walked in. They were standing beside the marble fireplace, talking to a man who looked all too familiar. Ellie recognized him immediately. He was the driver of the red sports car.

"Let me introduce you to my daughter," said the King.

"How divine," said the visitor. He stepped swiftly to Ellie's side, took her hand in his, and bowed theatrically. "Lord Leo of Vincent at your service, Your Highness."

"Hello," replied Ellie. She didn't say she was pleased to meet him, because she wasn't. She'd taken an instant dislike to the man when he'd frightened Angel.

The Queen was obviously much more enthusiastic about the new designer. "We're so lucky to have Lord Leo here," she declared in an excited voice. "He's related to Leonardo da Vinci."

"Who?" asked Ellie. She thought she'd heard the name before, but she couldn't remember where.

"Oh, dear," said the King. "I must ask Miss Stringle to spend more time on your art lessons. Leonardo da Vinci was one of the most famous artists who ever lived."

"And he's my great-great-great-great-great-grandfather," boasted Lord Leo. "I'm so lucky to have inherited his talent." He started to walk in a circle around Ellie, staring at her intently, as if she were an object in a museum. "How absolutely charming. I just love those curls, and that dress is so very, very . . ." He hesitated for a moment, as if searching for the right word.

"Pink?" suggested Ellie.

"That's it!" he cried, waving his hands dramatically in the air to emphasize his words. "It's so very pink. So absolutely, completely, and utterly pink."

The Queen beamed at him. "I'm so pleased that you like Aurelia's dress. I chose it for her myself." Then she turned to Ellie and said, "Lord Leo has exquisite taste. He's from such an important artistic family."

"Which is why he's the perfect person to be our royal designer," explained the King. "He agrees with me completely that we need to give the royal family a more modern look. So he's going to give us a makeover, just like they do on TV."

"Oh," said Ellie, trying to sound more enthusiastic than she felt. She wished her parents had never started watching those makeover TV shows. Ever since they had, they'd become convinced that the royal family needed to change its image.

Ellie wasn't sure she wanted her image changed by someone who dressed in such a peculiar way. Lord Leo was wearing a green velvet suit, green shoes, green socks, and a green silk shirt with ruffles around the neck. If he'd been smaller, he would have looked like a leprechaun. But he wasn't. He was so tall and thin that he looked more like a giant green bean.

The conversation was interrupted by the arrival of Higginbottom, who was carrying a large tray laden with cups and saucers, a silver teapot, and a plate of delicious cupcakes. Kate's grandmother had obviously been busy in the kitchen. She was the palace cook.

Lord Leo screwed up his face in dismay. "What *are* you wearing?" he asked, pointing to Higginbottom's evening suit. "Black is so last year."

"But butlers always wear black," said the King. "It's tradition."

"Nonsense," declared Lord Leo. "Traditions can be changed. If you want to bring the royal family up to date, you've got to let go of the past."

"Are you sure?" asked the Queen.

"Absolutely," said Lord Leo. "You can't have a makeover without change."

To Ellie's surprise, the King and Queen nodded in agreement. Lord Leo seemed to know exactly what to say to persuade them, and they were obviously impressed by the fact that he was related to Leonardo da Vinci.

That gave Ellie an idea. "Is pink last year, too?" she asked. Maybe, she thought, he could persuade her parents to redecorate her very pink bedroom.

"Absolutely not!" gushed the designer. "Pink is perfection, especially for princesses."

Ellie's shoulders sagged with disappointment. She'd liked the idea of a pink bedroom when she was small, but she didn't really like it anymore. She was trying to persuade her parents to paint her room purple. Lord Leo's opinion would make that task much harder.

She reached for a cupcake to cheer herself up and gazed through the window while nibbling the icing. The red sports car was parked outside. Its license plate said LEO 1.

Ellie scowled at it. Her parents obviously thought Lord Leo was charming, but she didn't. He was a bad driver, he had bad taste, and he knew nothing at all about ponies. What sort of mess was he going to make of her home?

Chapter 3

The next morning, Ellie was relieved to find that everything in the palace looked the same as usual. Lord Leo hadn't begun to make any changes yet. She smiled and tried to convince herself that a makeover might not be such a bad thing.

Her smile disappeared, however, when she arrived for her morning lesson. Miss Stringle told her to write a story without any ponies in it. How interesting could a story without ponies possibly be? Ellie chewed the end of her pencil thoughtfully and stared out of the window as she tried to come up with ideas.

She couldn't see the royal stable from where she was sitting, but she did see a bright yellow delivery van arrive at the palace. The words *Fantastic Fashions for the Fabulous* were painted in bright blue on the side of the van.

"I wonder what's in there," muttered Ellie.

"It's probably something to do with that dreadful man," replied Miss Stringle as she peered out of the window.

Ellie stared at her in surprise. "Don't you like Lord Leo?" she asked.

"I certainly don't like his ideas," said Miss Stringle. "Royalty is not supposed to change. It's supposed to stay the same. So should palaces, and so should governesses."

Ellie smiled. "Has he tried to change you?"

"Scarlet!" Miss Stringle spat the word out as if it were something dreadful-tasting. "He wants me to wear *scarlet*. I told him that generations of palace governesses have always worn brown. But he insisted that brown was . . ."

". . . So last year?" suggested Ellie.

"Exactly!" agreed Miss Stringle. "And I don't care if he's right. Last year is perfectly fine for me. I don't even mind last century."

"I don't like him much, either," Ellie said quietly.

Her governess smiled. "It's good to see we've found something that we agree on, my dear." Then she hastily added, "But we must be polite to Lord Leo." She peered down at the blank piece of paper on Ellie's desk. "Maybe I've been a little unfair to you this morning. I still don't want you to write about ponies, but I suppose I don't mind a few unicorns."

Ideas immediately flooded into Ellie's mind. Soon, she was so busy writing about a magical world of unicorns that she was surprised when Miss Stringle told her to stop for lunch.

Ellie got an even bigger surprise when she arrived in the dining room. The maid who opened the door wasn't in her usual uniform. Instead of a black dress, she was wearing a shimmery purple one. Its long skirt was so tight that she was finding it hard to walk. Ellie guessed that Fantastic Fashions for the Fabulous probably had something to do with the change in uniform.

The maid tried to curtsy, but the dress didn't allow her to bend her knees properly, and she nearly fell over. "Oops!" she cried. "I'm afraid I haven't gotten the hang of this yet. Excuse me, Your Highness."

"It's okay, Susan," said Ellie. She felt sorry for the maid. She looked so uncomfortable.

Ellie saw her parents already sitting at the table, deep in conversation.

The Queen looked up as Ellie sat down in her usual place. "Doesn't Susan's new uniform look fantastic?" she said.

"Are all the maids wearing purple now?" asked Ellie. She was glad that Lord Leo wasn't there. This was the first chance she'd had to speak to her parents in privacy since he had arrived.

"Not at all," the King replied, beaming. "Lord Leo has put all the maids in different colors. When they line up side by side, they look like a rainbow. It's wonderful."

"Are you sure?" asked Ellie. Then she

added in a whisper, "Susan doesn't look very happy in her new outfit."

"Oh, dear," said the Queen in a concerned voice. "I do hope she'll get used to it soon. Lord Leo promised us that everyone would."

"I'm not sure I will," said Ellie. "I wish you wouldn't let Lord Leo change everything."

"Nonsense," said the King. "You heard what he said. Change is good. Change is exciting. We can't go on living in the past forever."

"And Lord Leo really is a great designer," added the Queen. "He's related to one of the greatest artists in history."

Ellie realized there was no point in arguing with them. They had obviously made up

their minds and seemed completely capti-
vated by Lord Leo. So she walked across the
room to choose her lunch from the selection
of dishes laid out on the serving table. There
were rolls of ham stuffed with cream cheese,
chicken breasts roasted with truffles, and
some delicate meringue swans swimming on
a sea of thick chocolate sauce.

"What would you like to eat, Your
Highness?" asked a man wearing a bright
red jacket, white pants, and shiny red
boots that reached his knees.

Ellie stared in astonishment. It was
Higginbottom, the butler. "You look so
different," she said. "I hardly recognized you."

Higginbottom looked a little embar-
rassed. "I hardly recognize myself," he

muttered. "I look more like a lion tamer than a butler."

Ellie tried not to giggle. He was right. His outfit looked as if it had come straight from the circus. But she couldn't imagine him telling an angry lion how to behave. He'd have been more likely to offer it a sandwich.

"Do you think you'll get used to it?" Ellie asked, wondering if her mother was right.

"I suppose I will," answered Higginbottom. "But that doesn't mean I'll ever like it."

Ellie felt sorry for him and for all the maids. They didn't like Lord Leo's changes, and neither did she. If only there were something she could do to stop him.

Chapter 4

After lunch, Ellie went back to finish her unicorn story. As soon as Miss Stringle let her go later that afternoon, she rushed down to the royal stable. Meg had promised to give her a riding lesson, and she was eager to get started. She also wanted to tell Kate about Lord Leo, but, to her disappointment, her friend wasn't waiting for her.

"Maybe the bus was late," suggested Meg.

Kate lived at the palace with her grandparents, but she went to school in a different town.

Meg picked up a big box of grooming supplies. "Let's get Sundance ready while we're waiting. I'm going to give you a lunging lesson today."

Ellie was confused. She knew that lunging was a way to exercise a pony without getting on its back, but she couldn't see the point of doing it when she and Kate both wanted to ride. "I thought we were having a riding lesson," she said.

"You are," Meg replied with a laugh. She held out a very long rope. "I'll fasten one end of this lunging rein to Sundance and hold the other end in my hand. Then I'll make him go around me in a circle while you just concentrate on your riding."

Ellie was pleased that she would be riding after all, but she was worried that it might not be as easy as Meg made it sound. So she focused all her attention on grooming Sundance and tried not to think about what was coming next. Soon the chestnut pony's coat was gleaming, and his hooves shone from being oiled. Ellie got his saddle and bridle and put them on. "There's still no sign of Kate," she said.

"We'd better start without her," said Meg. She picked up a halter with three large brass rings attached to the noseband. "This is called the cavesson," she explained as she fastened it to the top of Sundance's bridle. Then she attached the lunging rein to one of the rings and started to lead the chestnut pony out of the yard.

Ellie got her riding hat from the tack room and followed Meg and Sundance. She caught up to them just as they reached the sand school on the other side of the barn. The sand school was a large rectangular area surrounded by a wooden fence. The thick layer of sand that covered the ground made it soft enough for the ponies to walk on whatever the weather.

Meg waited while Ellie swung herself

into the saddle. Then she tied the reins in a knot. "That will keep them out of the way," she explained. "You won't be needing them today." She instructed Sundance to walk forward and used the lunging rein to guide him so that he went around her in a large circle.

Ellie felt strange not being in control while riding. She remembered her very first riding lessons, when George, the old groom, used to lead her on Shadow. But even then, she had held on to the reins. Now she wasn't quite sure what to do with her hands.

"Put your arms out to the side," called Meg. "I want you to concentrate on balance today." She urged Sundance into a trot.

Ellie tried to rise up and down in the saddle, to move in time with the pony's feet. She was surprised at how much more difficult it was when she didn't have her hands in front of her. But Meg was right. Not having to worry about controlling Sundance made it easier to think about what her legs and body were doing.

Around and around they went, first in one direction and then in the other. Each time they turned toward the palace, Ellie looked eagerly for a glimpse of Kate. Surely she would come soon. She wasn't usually this late.

Finally, as she was practicing cantering without stirrups, Ellie spotted her friend running toward the sand school. She grinned and waved at her merrily, but Kate didn't wave back. She didn't look very happy.

Meg stopped Sundance, and Ellie jumped off and rushed up to Kate. "Is everything okay?' she asked.

"I'm okay, but my grandma isn't. I've been trying to calm her down," Kate explained. "She's really upset. One of the maids fell over because of the silly dress she was wearing, and she dropped a really special chocolate cake that had taken Grandma a really long time to make."

"It's all Lord Leo's fault," grumbled Ellie.

"He's upsetting everyone."

"Except your parents," said Kate.

Ellie sighed. "They think he's wonderful. He's convinced them that everyone will like his changes in the end."

"Grandma won't, and neither will Grand-dad," declared Kate. "They liked things the way they were. If everything's going to change like this, they're not sure they want to stay at the palace anymore."

Ellie stared at her in dismay. "But they can't leave. If they go, you'll go, too."

"I know," cried Kate. "And I don't want to."

Ellie blinked back her tears. She had been so lonely before Kate came to live at the palace. If her friend went away, there'd be no one to play with and no one to share her ponies with. That thought gave Ellie new resolve. "We can't let that happen," she insisted. "We've got to do something to stop Lord Leo."

Chapter 5

Sundance nudged Ellie's arm with his nose and then did the same to Kate. "He's telling you both to cheer up," Meg said, smiling. "Now, stop worrying, and try to enjoy the rest of your lesson."

"It's Kate's turn to ride," said Ellie. She didn't mind watching for a while. She'd worked so hard that she was glad to have a break.

But she wasn't able to rest for long. After Kate had practiced walking and trotting in a circle, Meg called Ellie into the center of the circle. "Now it's time for you to learn to lunge," she said. "It can be a very useful skill."

Ellie hesitated. Part of her was eager to try holding the lunging rein, but the rest of her was nervous. "Suppose something goes wrong?" she asked.

"You'll be fine," said Meg. "Sundance is very calm and sensible. He's the perfect pony to learn with."

"And besides, I'm still on him," added Kate. "If anything happens, I can pick up the reins and ride him normally."

Meg showed Ellie how to hold the lunging rein in one hand and the whip in the other. "Now, use your voice to control him, just like you do with Shadow when he's pulling the carriage."

"Walk on, Sundance!" called Ellie, trying not to let her nervousness show. Sundance stepped forward obediently, walking in a large circle with Ellie at the center. She had to turn to keep facing him as he walked around. If she hadn't, she would have ended up with the lunging rein wrapped around her.

Sundance behaved very well, and Ellie's confidence grew quickly. Soon, she had the pony trotting and cantering in circles while Kate practiced riding without reins.

Ellie was concentrating so hard that she didn't notice she'd attracted an audience until she heard her mother call, "Aurelia!"

She stopped Sundance and led him over to the fence, where the King and Queen were standing with Lord Leo. He was wearing what Ellie decided must have been his walking-in-the-country outfit: green jacket, green shirt, green designer jeans, and green Wellington boots.

"We're just showing Lord Leo the palace grounds," explained the King.

"Are you planning to make changes out here, too?" asked Ellie. She didn't want him upsetting Meg in addition to everyone else.

"No, of course not," Lord Leo replied. "There's way too much to do inside."

"Lord Leo's been telling us all about his wonderful home in the country," said the Queen. "You two girls might be interested. He has horses."

Ellie looked at him in surprise. This was the man who had frightened Angel with his car. How could someone who owned horses have been so insensitive toward her pony? "Could you please tell us about them?" she asked, curious to figure Lord Leo out.

"Oh, no!" replied Lord Leo. "I wouldn't dream of boring you."

"I can listen to people talk about horses for hours," said Ellie.

"So can I," said Kate, still perched on

Sundance's back. "What are their names?"

Lord Leo hesitated, as if he were having trouble remembering. "Now let me think. Um . . . er . . . there's Dobbin, and Rover, and Misty, and Black Beauty."

Ellie's curiosity grew. She had never heard such unimaginative names. She'd once had a rocking horse called Dobbin, and Rover sounded like a better name for a dog. But she decided not to say anything. She wanted to find out more. "What color are they?" she asked.

This time Lord Leo seemed more confident. "Black Beauty's black, of course. Misty is white. And Rover is exactly the same shade of brown as this pretty little pony."

Before he had time to describe Dobbin, his cell phone started playing the national anthem. He pulled it out of his pocket and read the message on the screen. Then he smiled apologetically at the King and Queen and announced, "I'm terribly sorry, Your Majesties. I have to cut our expedition short to make a few arrangements for tomorrow."

Ellie watched him walk back to the palace, along with her parents. Then she turned to Kate and asked, "How could anyone with horses have trouble remembering their names?"

"Or call Sundance brown, instead of chestnut?" replied Kate. She looked thoughtful. "Maybe he doesn't really know anything about horses. That would explain why he frightened Angel yesterday."

"But that would mean he's making it all up," said Ellie. "And if he's lying about the horses, maybe he's lying about other things as well."

Chapter 6

The more Ellie and Kate thought about Lord Leo, the more suspicious they became.

"Maybe he doesn't even know that much about design," suggested Kate. "That would explain why the new staff uniforms are so awful."

Ellie nodded thoughtfully. "He's probably not related to Leonardo da Vinci, either."

"But why would he lie about that?" asked Kate.

Ellie shrugged. "Maybe he likes to sound important. It certainly works. That's why Mom and Dad trust him so much."

Kate's eyes brightened. "You have to tell them. If they find out he's lying, they might send him away, and everything will go back to normal."

Ellie was sure her friend was right. But she didn't have a chance to speak to her parents alone until later that evening. She waited until Lord Leo was distracted looking at some oil paintings in the corridor. Then she crept into the parlor without letting him see her.

The King and Queen were sitting in their comfy thrones, sipping tea from china cups while they played chess. They looked up in surprise when Ellie came tiptoeing in. "Is everything okay?" asked the Queen.

Ellie shook her head. "I need to talk to you about Lord Leo."

"Not that again," complained the King. "You've already made it quite clear that you don't like what he's doing."

"We understand how you feel, Aurelia,"

added the Queen, with a sympathetic smile. "Lord Leo has explained that little children always resist change at first."

Ellie felt a wave of anger. "I'm not a little child!" she cried. Then she forced herself to calm down and added in a quieter voice, "He's lying about having horses."

The King slowly lowered his cup onto his saucer and stared at her. "That's a very serious thing to say, Aurelia. I hope you can prove it."

"Of course I can," declared Ellie. "First of all, he had trouble remembering his horses' names, and then he said Sundance was brown, instead of chestnut."

"That sounds perfectly reasonable to me," said the Queen. "I have trouble remembering names all the time. And he's a very fashionable man, so it's natural for him to use modern names for colors rather than the traditional horsey ones."

The King gave Ellie a reassuring hug. "There's nothing to worry about. Your mother and I know what we're doing, and so does Lord Leo. The whole palace is going to have a wonderful new image."

Ellie sighed. She knew she wasn't going to persuade them. But she was positive she was right. The designer wasn't telling the truth, and she was determined to find out why.

The next morning was Saturday, so Ellie didn't have to go to class. But no one else seemed to be taking the day off. The palace was abuzz with activity. All the maids were

hobbling about in their new dresses, trying
to cover the carpets with dust sheets.

Ellie spotted Higginbottom in the
entrance hall. He was still wearing his lion-
tamer outfit.

She crept up behind him, planning to
roar fiercely and make him jump. But at the
last minute, she changed her mind. He was
already so upset that it didn't seem fair to

make fun of him. Instead, she just asked, "What's going on?"

The butler smiled and bowed slightly. "It's Lord Leo again, Your Highness. His men will be here any minute to start the decorating."

Ellie looked around. Apart from the dust sheets, the palace looked exactly the same as it always did. "But you're not ready yet. You've still got to take all the paintings down, put the ornaments away, and move the furniture."

Higginbottom sighed. "Apparently Lord Leo and his staff are going to move everything. We weren't supposed to do anything at all. But I insisted on the dust sheets. I don't want their dirty feet trampling all over our clean carpets."

As he finished speaking, an enormous

truck drove up to the palace entrance. A group of men in brown overalls got out and swung open the large doors at the back. Just then, Lord Leo drove up beside them. His red sports car sent up a spray of gravel as it screeched to a halt.

He jumped out and started issuing orders. Then he noticed Ellie watching him from the doorway, and his voice dropped to a whisper. The men huddled around him so they could hear.

As soon as Lord Leo had finished speaking with them, the men set to work unloading a variety of boxes, ladders, and cans of paint. Soon there were men everywhere, carrying things in and out of the palace. They seemed especially interested in all the ornaments and pictures. They peered at the signatures on the paintings and lifted up the silver statues to read the hall-marks on their bases. One of them even used a magnifying glass, so that he could examine them in detail.

There's something about them I don't trust, thought Ellie. She had never seen workmen behave like that before. But she couldn't go to her parents again with just a suspicion. Somehow she had to find out what Lord Leo and his men were up to.

Chapter 7

"Are you sure this is going to work?" asked Kate, as she led Angel toward the enormous truck.

"It's the only way," said Ellie. "We need to keep an eye on what they're doing, and Angel is the perfect excuse."

Angel arched her neck and flared her nostrils as she stared curiously at the truck. Kate stroked the foal's face to reassure her. "It's all right," she whispered. "It's not going to hurt you."

"It's only a truck," added Ellie. She patted Angel's neck and felt the foal relax. Then she turned to Kate and said, "Don't stop. We need to get closer so we can see better."

They led Angel around the back of the large vehicle. Lord Leo was still there, supervising his men as they moved things in and out of the palace. As the girls arrived, one of the workmen stomped into the truck carrying two cans of paint. His heavy footsteps made so much noise on the wooden ramp that Angel stepped back in surprise.

"Steady, girl," said Ellie soothingly.

Lord Leo spun around to see who was talking. A brief look of annoyance showed on his face, but he immediately replaced it with a wide smile. "Good morning, Princess Aurelia. I'm surprised you're not out riding on such a wonderful day."

Ellie smiled back, trying hard to give the impression of complete innocence. "We're giving Angel a lesson," she explained. "Walking her by your truck is the perfect way to teach her to be confident in traffic."

"It's very useful practice," added Kate. "You've already seen how nervous she is."

"Of course, of course," replied Lord Leo. He waved a hand at them dismissively. "But do try to stay out of everyone's way."

Ellie and Kate turned Angel away from the truck and led her around in a large circle. As they walked, Ellie whispered, "Did you see what that man was carrying?"

"Cans of paint," said Kate. "But there's nothing strange about that. He's a decorator."

"But why would he be carrying them *into* the truck?" asked Ellie. "They've only just been carried out of it."

Kate scratched her head thoughtfully with the end of Angel's lead rope. "Maybe it was the wrong color."

That explanation made sense, but Ellie didn't want to admit that it might be true. She preferred to think that she and Kate might have stumbled on an amazing plot, the way the children in her pony books always did. "There's only one way to find out the truth," replied Ellie. "We'll have to put the rest of our plan into action."

They walked Angel around in another large circle while they waited for the right moment. It came when Lord Leo went back inside the palace, taking three of the men with him. With fewer people around, there would be less chance of getting caught.

"Now," whispered Ellie. She slipped away from Kate and Angel and pressed herself flat against the far side of the truck, where she couldn't be seen from the palace. She crossed her fingers tightly, hoping no one would walk around and see her hiding there.

A few seconds later, Kate let out a loud, remarkably convincing cry of pain. Ellie peered around the corner of the truck and saw everyone turning to look at her friend. Kate was hopping up and down on one foot, in a wonderful imitation of some-one who had just been stepped on by a pony.

Ellie knew this was her chance. No one was looking at the truck. She summoned all her courage, tiptoed up the ramp, and crept inside. It was darker than she'd expected, and the stuffy air was tinged with the sharp scents of wood and paint. The floor was covered with a mess of boxes and packages; close to one wall stood the two paint cans that the mover had carried in. At least, she thought they were the same cans. They'd been set down off to the side, away from the other decorating supplies.

Ellie picked up one of the cans and shook it gently. An excited thrill ran down her spine as she heard something rattle inside— something that definitely wasn't paint. With her heart racing, she picked up a screwdriver from the floor and started to remove the lid.

Suddenly she heard a footstep on the ramp and froze in fear. Someone was coming into the truck. Now she was in real trouble.

Chapter 8

Ellie struggled to stay calm. She and Kate had known she might get caught. That was why they'd planned her next step carefully. But whether or not it would work depended on how good she was at acting.

She put down the screwdriver and stood up quietly as the footsteps came closer. She had to fight back her natural instinct to run away or hide. Either of those actions would have instantly made her look guilty.

Instead, she peered behind a large box and called, "Here, kitty, kitty, kitty!"

"What are you doing in here?" shouted someone with a deep voice.

She swung around and saw a large man blocking her way out of the truck. Her stomach contracted in fear, but she knew she couldn't show it. She smiled as innocently as she could and said, "I'm look-ing for the cat."

"What cat?" asked the man.

"The one that frightened Angel and made her step on Kate's foot," Ellie explained. "I saw it run in here, and I thought I should get it out before you drive away."

To her surprise, the man smiled. "That's very sweet of you, my dear. But you'd better leave that to me. Now, run along. We can't have you climbing around in here getting hurt. We would never hear the end of it from your parents."

Ellie did as she was told, delighted that her plan had worked so well. As soon as she was outside she ran to join Kate, who was limping convincingly toward the royal stable with Angel. They could hear the man inside the truck calling, "Here, little kitty. Come on, don't be shy."

Kate giggled. "I can't believe that worked. I was so scared when I saw him going up the ramp."

"So was I," said Ellie. "But we still haven't figured out what's going on. There was definitely something in one of those cans that was not paint. But I didn't have time to see what it was."

Kate groaned. "Oh, Ellie, please don't say I have to pretend that Angel stepped on me again."

Ellie knew Kate was right. They couldn't try the same trick twice. But there must be some way to prove to her parents that Lord Leo was up to no good.

By lunchtime, the palace had been almost completely cleared. All the paintings and ornaments in the entrance hall had already disappeared. Ellie wondered how many of them were in storage and how many were hidden in the truck.

Lord Leo was in high spirits during the

meal. Dressed in green as usual, he boasted about his wonderful home, his yacht, and his private plane. As he spoke, he waved his hands around dramatically to empha-size his words, making things extremely difficult for the maids who were serving the food.

"And the house is surrounded by beauti-ful countryside," he declared, swinging both arms wide. His left hand narrowly missed the coffeepot Higginbottom was carrying, but Lord Leo didn't seem to notice.

"It must be perfect for riding," said the Queen.

"Oh, yes," he gushed. "I ride every day when I'm at home."

Liar, thought Ellie. Then she had an idea.

If she couldn't prove Lord Leo was making things up, perhaps she could get him to prove it himself. "Perhaps you'd like a ride on one of my ponies while you're here," she suggested.

But Lord Leo wasn't going to be trapped that easily. "What a kind offer," he said with a smug smile. "It's such a pity your ponies are too small for me."

"But they're not," replied Ellie. "Starlight's much bigger than the others. She could carry you easily."

"Oh," said Lord Leo. His smile vanished for a moment, and he seemed at a loss for words. Then he smirked again and said, "I'd love to ride her, but unfortunately I've left all my riding clothes at home."

To Ellie's delight, the King patted Lord

Leo on the shoulder and declared, "Not a problem. After all you've done for us, I wouldn't dream of letting you miss your ride over such a small matter."

He called out to Higginbottom. "Take the royal car to town, and buy Lord Leo the best riding outfit you can find."

"Certainly, Your Majesty," replied the butler. He bowed deeply and left. On the way out, he glanced at Ellie, and she was surprised to see a hint of mischief in his eyes.

"You must have your ride this afternoon," the Queen said to Lord Leo. "You're working so hard that you deserve a break."

"Thank you," said Lord Leo in a very quiet voice. He seemed to have lost his usual confidence, and his face was starting to look almost as green as his outfit.

Ellie slipped quietly away from the table. She had to get ready. If her plan was going to work, this would have to be a very special ride.

Chapter 9

Ellie and Kate groomed Starlight until her coat shone. Then they brushed all the tangles out of her mane and tail and made sure there wasn't a speck of mud on the long, shaggy hairs that hung over her hooves.

Kate pointed at them and smiled. "I bet Lord Leo doesn't even know they're called feathers."

"I can't complain about that," Ellie said,

chuckling. "I didn't know either until Meg told me." She heard the crunch of tires on the drive. "That sounds like Higginbottom coming back. I'll go and check."

She ran over to the palace and caught up with the butler just as he met Lord Leo in the entrance hall.

Higginbottom bowed respectfully and handed over a large box. It was covered with gold wrapping; the words *Fantastic Fashions for the Fabulous* were printed across the top in familiar blue writing.

Lord Leo put on a reasonably convincing show of gratitude. But as he pulled each item out of the box, he looked more and more dismayed. None of the clothes were green. The jacket and jodhpurs were bright orange, and so was the silk cover for the riding hat.

He glared at Higginbottom. "Why did you get them in orange?" he snapped. "You must know I love green. Isn't it obvious?"

The butler's face lit up with a smile of satisfaction. "But green is so last year," he purred.

Ellie clapped her hand over her mouth to keep herself from laughing. Lord Leo looked stunned. Before he had time to say anything, however, the King and Queen swept into the hall, and his expression changed to a forced grin.

The King beamed back. "Good. I see your outfit's arrived." He turned and smiled at Ellie. "Should Lord Leo meet you at the stable, Aurelia?"

"No, the sand school would be better," replied Ellie. "Why don't you both come and watch?"

"What an excellent idea," said the Queen.

"Please don't feel you have to," suggested Lord Leo, with a hint of desperation in his voice. "I wouldn't be at all offended if you didn't."

"I know you wouldn't," said the King, "but it will give us great pleasure to see you enjoying yourself."

When she got back to the stable, Ellie found that Kate had already put Starlight's saddle and bridle on. So she got the cavesson from the tack room, adjusted it to fit the bay mare's head, and fastened it in place.

Meg attached the lunging rein and handed it to Ellie. "Just remember everything I've taught you. Starlight's as good as gold when she's lunged. You shouldn't have any problems."

They arrived at the sand school at the same time as the royal party. The King and Queen were in the lead, followed by two footmen carrying folding thrones, a rainbow of maids carrying refreshments, and Higginbottom. The butler wasn't carrying anything. Ellie suspected he was there just to watch the fun.

Lord Leo walked just behind the King and Queen. The forced grin was still on his face, but his shoulders drooped miserably inside his orange jacket.

Kate nudged Ellie with her elbow. "He looks like a giant carrot," she whispered.

Ellie giggled. "I hope Starlight isn't too hungry." Carrots were the pony's favorite treat.

She stepped forward and welcomed Lord Leo into the sand school. "I thought we'd start you off on the lunge," she explained, holding up the lunging rein to show what she was talking about. "That'll give you a chance to get used to Starlight."

She thought she detected a glimmer of relief in his eyes as he realized he'd be led. That swiftly vanished, though, when she continued, "Then we can go for a good gallop across the deer park and do some jumping on our cross-country course."

Lord Leo gulped, but he managed to keep the grin on his face. "I suppose I'd better get on," he said, walking around to Starlight's right side.

Kate gave a polite cough. "Wouldn't you prefer to mount from the left?" she asked.

"Of course," he replied quickly. He gave Starlight's neck a nervous pat and moved to the pony's other side, muttering, "I was just checking to see if all the stirrupy things were there."

Meg hurried over carrying a large box. "Perhaps you'd like to use a mounting block," she suggested. Then she turned to Ellie and whispered, "He doesn't seem to know what he's doing. I don't think you'll get him on without it."

Lord Leo climbed on to the box and put his right foot in the stirrup. For a wonderful

moment, Ellie thought he was going to end up sitting backward on Starlight, facing the pony's tail. But he didn't. After a moment's thought, he took his right foot out again, put his left foot in instead, and swung himself into the saddle the right way.

That was the only thing he did right. His toes pointed down, while his heels pointed up. His back slumped like a sack of potatoes, and he held the reins so high that he looked like a dog begging for a treat.

Ellie realized with delight that her suspicions were correct. Lord Leo had absolutely no idea how to ride. If her plan worked properly, he would be in even more trouble when Starlight started to move. The King and Queen would be sure to notice that he didn't know what he was doing. Then they would have to believe that he hadn't told them the truth.

Chapter 10

Ellie gently pried the reins from Lord Leo's fingers and tied them in a knot. "You won't need those for a while," she explained.

He immediately transferred his grip to the front of the saddle. "Fine," he squeaked, in a strangely high-pitched voice. His grin was now frozen on his face, and his teeth stayed clamped together even when he spoke.

Ellie took the lunging rein in one hand and the whip in the other. Then she stepped away from Starlight and made the bay mare walk around in a large circle. It seemed fair to give Lord Leo a chance to get his balance.

After a few steps, he seemed to realize that sitting on a walking horse wasn't very difficult. He began to look more confident. He relaxed his grin and let go of the saddle.

A small crowd had gathered beside the sand school. The men from the truck had abandoned their work and drifted over to see what was happening. Miss Stringle had come, too, and so had several of the palace guards. The King and Queen smiled and waved as Lord Leo rode past.

Ellie waited until Lord Leo was in the middle of waving back. Then she urged

Starlight into a bouncy trot.

"Oooh!" Lord Leo squealed as he grabbed hold of the saddle again.

"It's a good thing you can already ride," called Ellie. "Trotting is so uncomfortable if you can't."

"I know," cried Lord Leo. His bottom bumped painfully around in the saddle, because he didn't know how to rise up and down in time with Starlight's feet. The pony trotted around and around, faster and faster. The quicker she went, the harder Lord Leo bumped up and down in the saddle. Soon his back sagged in exhaustion, and the fake grin finally disappeared from his face. "Can we stop now?" he cried.

"Not yet!" called Ellie. "We've only just begun." She urged Starlight into a canter.

The sudden change of pace knocked the designer off balance. His left foot slipped out of its stirrup, and he slid sideways in the saddle. "Oh, no!" he wailed.

The King leaped to his feet. "Lord Leo's in trouble. Slow the pony down, Aurelia."

Ellie did as she was told. Starlight obediently stopped cantering and started to trot again.

But that didn't help Lord Leo. He bumped around harder than ever. He gripped the saddle so hard that his knuckles turned white. "Please, stop!" he begged.

"In a minute," Ellie promised. "But first I think you have something to tell my parents."

Lord Leo slipped further out of the saddle. He threw his arms around Starlight's neck to save himself and stared desperately at Ellie. "I don't know what you mean," he cried.

"Just tell everyone the truth," said Ellie.

Lord Leo was clinging on to Starlight like a monkey, and he looked ready to burst into tears. "Okay, okay," he wailed. "I'm not really related to Leonardo da Vinci. I'm not even a real designer."

Most of those in the crowd gasped in astonishment. The only ones who didn't react were the workmen. They started to creep quietly back to the truck, but soon found their way blocked by the palace guards.

The King ignored them. He was busy concentrating on Lord Leo. "Who are you, then?" he demanded.

Ellie brought Starlight to a halt and watched the fake designer slide off and collapse in the sand. Then she pointed at him and declared, "He's a thief. I'm sure he is. Just look inside his truck and see."

"We certainly will," agreed the Queen, her eyes wide with shock. "Guards, bring that man, and follow us." She walked briskly back in the direction of the palace with the King. Two of the guards lifted Lord Leo to his feet and marched him along after them.

Ellie and Kate followed close behind with Starlight.

As soon as they reached the truck, Ellie jumped inside and found the can she'd tried to open earlier. She held it up and shook it. "Listen," she said. "Paint doesn't rattle like that."

The sergeant of the palace guard drew his ornamental sword and used it to pry the lid off the can. Ellie watched him anxiously. Suppose she was wrong? Suppose Lord Leo wasn't a thief and all that was inside was a screwdriver?

As soon as the lid was off, she leaned forward and reached inside the can. To her relief, she didn't find a screwdriver. Instead, her fingers closed around an object that felt very familiar. She pulled it out and saw that she was right. It was her favorite statue—the flying horse—looking more beautiful than ever as it glittered in the sunlight.

Ellie thrust it triumphantly into her father's hands and declared, "There's the proof."

The King waved the statue angrily at Lord

Leo. "You're under arrest. Your scheme has failed."

"I know," muttered Lord Leo. He looked utterly miserable as the palace guards led him away.

The King smiled sheepishly at Ellie. "I'm sorry we didn't believe you before."

"It's okay. But are we still going to update the image of the royal family?" asked Ellie. "I think I've had enough change to last me for a long time."

"So have I," laughed the Queen.

The King laughed, too. "Maybe a royal makeover isn't as important as I thought." He turned to the servants and announced, "I think we'll go back to the old uniforms. From now on, we'll stick to tradition."

"Yay!" said Kate. "Grandma and Granddad

will be very glad to hear that."

"Which means you won't have to move," said Ellie, smiling at her friend. She felt very happy. Everything was back the way it had been—or would be, as soon as Higginbottom stopped looking like a lion tamer.

The King put his arm around Ellie's shoulders. "We're very proud of you," he said.

"You've saved the palace treasure," added the Queen.

"Thanks," said Ellie, "but I couldn't have done it without Kate." Then she pulled a carrot out of her pocket and gave it to the bay mare. "Or Starlight," she added.

Here's a sneak peek at the next adventure
of the

Pony-Crazed Princess

in

Princess Ellie's Snowy Ride

Princess Ellie's Snowy Ride

Chapter 1

"Wow!" squealed Princess Ellie. "Look at those mountains."

"They're so huge," said her best friend, Kate. "And look, they've even got snow on the top."

"Of course they do," said Miss Stringle. "Andirovia is a much colder country than ours. Now, stop pressing your face against the car window, Princess Aurelia. That's no way to behave. We can't have the public thinking princesses have squashed noses."

Ellie groaned as she sat back in her seat. She hated it when her governess called her by her real name. But she was too excited about going on a royal vacation to stay miserable for long. This was the first time she had ever visited her friend Prince John and his family. She had never been to Andirovia before. She gazed longingly at the white mountain peaks. "I've never seen real snow close up."

To find out what happens next, read

Princess Ellie's Snowy Ride